THE TERRIBLE
HODAG

WRITTEN BY
CAROLINE ARNOLD

ILLUSTRATED BY
LAMBERT DAVIS

HARCOURT BRACE JOVANOVICH, PUBLISHERS

SAN DIEGO   NEW YORK   LONDON

HBJ

Library of Congress Cataloging-in-Publication Data
Arnold, Caroline.
The terrible Hodag / by Caroline Arnold; illustrated by Lambert Davis.
p.   cm.
Summary: A logger named Ole Swenson befriends
the terrible Hodag who helps him run
the boss man out of the forest.
ISBN 0-15-284750-2
[1. Folklore — United States.]   I. Davis, Lambert, ill.
II. Title.
PZ8.1.A729Te 1989
398.2′0973 — dc19
[E]   88-18724

Printed in the United States of America
First edition
A B C D E

The illustrations in this book were done in acrylics on D'Arches 140-lb.
cold press watercolor paper.

The display type was set in Latin Bold.

The text type was set in Cochin.

Composition by Thompson Type, San Diego, California

Color separations were made by Bright Arts, Ltd., Hong Kong.

Printed by Holyoke Lithograph, Springfield, Massachusetts

Bound by Horowitz/Rae Book Manufacturers, Inc., Fairfield, New Jersey

Production supervision by Warren Wallerstein and Eileen McGlone

Designed by Michael Farmer

For my father, Lester Scheaffer, who
first told me the story of Ole Swenson
and the Hodag.

— C. A.

For the wild places and the wild things,
and the people who care about them.

— L. D.

STORYTELLER'S NOTE

It is possible that you have heard other stories about a mythical giant beast called the Hodag. Tales of this enormous creature are found in many regions of the United States. Like all stories that pass from one teller to the next, the details and exploits of the characters change often.

The first Hodag stories were told in logging camps. My story is based on tales told around summer campfires in the north woods of Wisconsin when I was a camper at Camp Bovey, formerly known as Camp Hodag. This version of Ole Swenson and the Hodag is a product of both memory and my own imagination.

IN THE FAR NORTH WOODS, a long time ago, there lived a lumberjack named Ole Swenson. No one else could swing an axe or pull a saw as fast as he could.

Each day, he and the other lumberjacks went into the forest to cut down trees. The *chop chop* of their axes echoed across the valley, and the buzz of their saws could be heard for miles.

"*Timber!*" they shouted as each tree crashed to the ground.

The men worked hard from sunup to sundown. But when night fell, they all went back to the lumbercamp. They did not want to meet the terrible Hodag.

When it was dark, the Hodag came out of his den.

The ground rumbled as he walked along the forest floor.

The Hodag's giant jaws opened wide as he gobbled whole bushes in single gulps.

In the morning, huge footsteps showed where he had walked, and whole clearings showed where he had eaten.

One day, the boss man of the lumbercamp came to Ole Swenson and said, "Winter is coming soon. You and your men have not cut enough trees."

"We're working as fast as we can," Ole Swenson told him.

"That's not fast enough," the boss man insisted. "I want you to cut down every single tree on the far hillside."

"But there are too many!" cried Ole Swenson.

"You could finish easily," the boss man snapped, "if you worked at night."

"No one will go into the forest at night," said Ole Swenson. "Everyone is afraid of the terrible Hodag."

"There is no such thing as a Hodag," the boss man scoffed. "Your men are just lazy. I want those trees cut by next Friday, or nobody gets paid."

Ole Swenson told the lumberjacks what the boss man had said. They were furious.

"There's never been a meaner man," said one.

"And we won't eat this winter if he doesn't pay us," said another.

"Then we'll have to work at night," Ole Swenson told them.

"Never," said the lumberjacks.

Ole Swenson did not know what to do.

I must come up with a plan, he thought. *Surely there is some way that we can cut those trees by Friday.*

Ole Swenson walked back to the edge of the forest. As night fell, it grew dark. He was thinking so hard he forgot to watch out for the Hodag.

Suddenly he looked up. Through the branches, he saw a giant red eye. Then he saw another red eye. They belonged to a huge creature. It had the head of an ox, the feet of a bear, the back of a dinosaur, and the tail of an alligator. Its eyes glowed like fire, and it was forty feet tall.

Ole Swenson screamed. "The Hodag!"

He jumped up and tried to run away, but he was so scared he couldn't move.

"Who are you?" a deep voice asked.

"I am Ole Swenson." He tried to be brave, but his voice shook. "You must be the Hodag."

When the huge beast opened its mouth to speak, Ole Swenson saw giant teeth, and huge puffs of smoke burst out of the creature's nose.

"Please don't eat me," begged Ole Swenson.

"Don't be afraid. I won't hurt you."

"Then why does everyone say that you are the terrible Hodag?" asked Ole Swenson.

"Nobody has ever dared to come close to me," said the Hodag. "No one is ever in the forest at night. What are *you* doing here?"

Ole Swenson told the Hodag about the mean boss man.

"I have seen him," said the Hodag, "and he is a selfish man. If he had his way, he would cut down the whole forest. Then I would have no place to live."

"He asks too much of us," Ole Swenson said. "My men will starve if they don't get paid."

The Hodag swished his tail to show how angry that made him. Five trees toppled to the ground behind him.

Suddenly Ole Swenson had an idea.

"Maybe you can help us," he said. He explained his plan, and the Hodag agreed. Then Ole Swenson climbed up onto the Hodag's spiny back. The Hodag walked through the forest, swishing his mighty tail from side to side.

Tree trunks splintered to the ground. By morning, the whole hillside was felled.

"Now the boss man will have to pay you," said the Hodag.

"Yes," said Ole Swenson. "Thank you."

Ole Swenson led the lumberjacks into the forest. They couldn't believe their eyes.

"We know you're strong," they said, "but this is amazing! How did you do it?"

"A friend helped me," Ole Swenson told them.

"Who is he?" asked the lumberjacks.

"I can't tell you now," replied Ole Swenson. "We have to get to work right away."

Soon the men were too busy to wonder about Ole Swenson's mysterious friend. All day they cut the branches off the trees and put logs into piles. It was hard work.

Then they brought the boss man to the forest. He saw the logs, but still he was not satisfied.

The lumberjacks were angry. "You promised to pay us," they all said at once.

"No," said the boss man. "You must take the logs to the sawmill by Friday. Then I will pay you."

"That's impossible!" they cried. "There are too many, and it will take forever!"

But the boss man would not listen. He did not want to pay them at all.

"Now we really will starve," the lumberjacks told Ole Swenson. "What are we going to do?"

"I'll try to think of a new plan."

Ole Swenson climbed to the top of a tall tree. From there he could see over the whole forest. On one side was the lumbercamp, and on the other was the sawmill. Far away to the south, Ole Swenson could see the train that carried lumber from the sawmill to the city. Fluffy clouds of smoke chugged out of the engine's smokestack. They reminded him of the Hodag.

Suddenly he had an idea.

"I think I know how we can do it," Ole Swenson said.

"How?" asked the men.

"First we must pile all the logs on carts."

"But who will take the carts to the sawmill?" the lumberjacks wanted to know.

"Leave it to me," said Ole Swenson.

When the carts were full the men went back to the lumbercamp. Ole Swenson stayed in the forest.

"Watch out for the Hodag," the lumberjacks warned.

"I will."

Ole Swenson set out on a long walk. As he got close to the Hodag's den, he felt the ground shake. Suddenly he saw the giant beast coming toward him. It had the head of an ox, the feet of a bear, the back of a dinosaur, and the tail of an alligator. It was the Hodag!

The Hodag lowered his huge head and stared at Ole Swenson with glowing red eyes.

"Did the boss man pay you?"

"Not yet," said Ole Swenson. "Now he says we must take all the logs to the sawmill."

"That man is too greedy!" the Hodag bellowed.

"Will you help us one more time?" Ole Swenson pleaded. He told him the plan, and once again the Hodag agreed.

Then Ole Swenson tied all the carts to the Hodag's tail. The Hodag pulled them through the forest to the sawmill. They finished at dawn. It was Friday.

"Wait for me at the edge of the forest," Ole Swenson told the Hodag. "I'll be back soon."

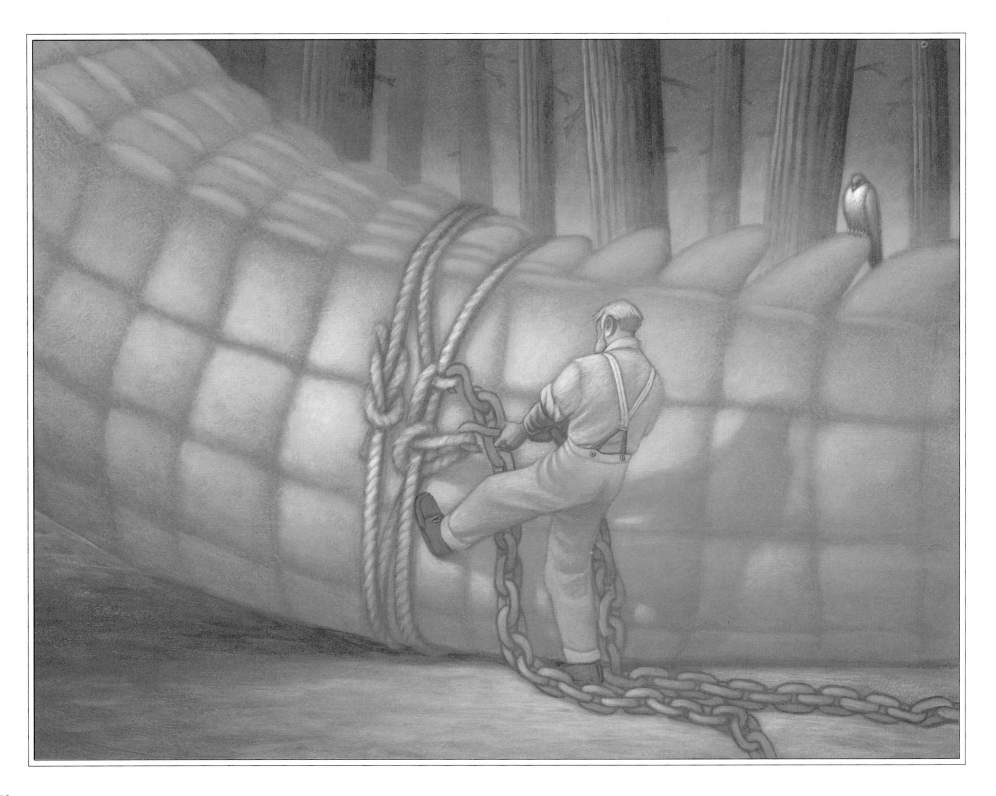

Ole Swenson went back to the camp. He got the men and led them to the sawmill.

"How on earth did you do it?" they asked.

"My friend helped me."

"This is a wonderful friend," said the lumberjacks. "We must thank him. Who *is* he?"

"He has the head of an ox, the feet of a bear, the back of a dinosaur, and the tail of an alligator. His eyes glow like fire, and he is forty feet tall."

"The terrible HODAG!" shouted the lumberjacks. "But we don't want to go near him. He'll eat us alive!"

"He isn't a terrible Hodag," said Ole Swenson. "Look how he has helped us."

Then one man stepped forward. "If Ole Swenson is not afraid of the Hodag, then we won't be afraid either."

So they all went into the forest to meet the Hodag.

"Hooray!" shouted the men. "Hooray for the Hodag!"

"If the boss man does not pay you now," said the Hodag, "just send him to me."

Ole Swenson and his men went back to the lumbercamp. They found the boss man and showed him that they had finished their job.

"You have tricked me," he said. "I won't pay you a penny until you tell me how you did it."

The lumberjacks smiled. "Come with us then," they said.

They took the boss man to the forest behind the sawmill. Suddenly the Hodag appeared. His huge red eyes flashed, and his giant steps sounded like thunder. The boss man was so scared he dropped all his money bags. Then he started to run. The boss man ran and ran and never came back. No one was sorry to see him go.

"Thank you," said Ole Swenson to the Hodag. "We would never have been paid without you."

Then he counted the money and divided it among the men.

"From now on," he said to the lumberjacks, "we will only cut the trees we need, and we will always be sure to leave part of the forest for the Hodag."

"You are a good man," said the Hodag.

Then the Hodag disappeared into the trees. No longer would the lumberjacks be afraid to go into the forest at night. Now they knew that the huge creature who had the head of an ox, the feet of a bear, the back of a dinosaur, and the tail of an alligator was their friend.